Can-Do
Crispies

Look out for more

Bake a Wish

books:

Feel Good Fairy Cakes

Get-Better Jelly

Feel Fearless Flapjacks

Bake a Wish

Can-Do Crispies

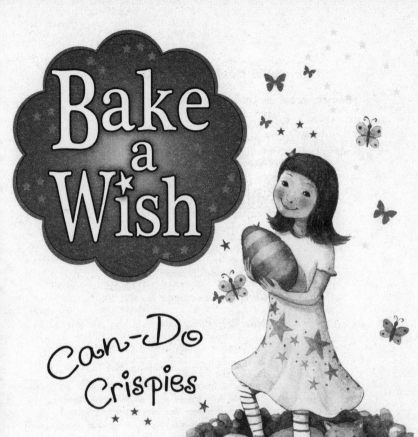

Lorna Honeywell

Illustrated by Samantha Chaffey

SCHOLASTIC

With special thanks to Pearl Morrison

First published in the UK in 2012 by Scholastic Children's Books
An imprint of Scholastic Ltd
Euston House, 24 Eversholt Street
London, NW1 1DB, UK
Registered office: Westfield Road, Southam, Warwickshire, CV47 0RA
SCHOLASTIC and associated logos are trademarks and/
or registered trademarks of Scholastic Inc.

Text copyright © Hothouse Fiction Limited, 2012
Illustrations copyright © Samantha Chaffey, 2012

The right of Lorna Honeywell and Samantha Chaffey to be identified as the
author and illustrator of this work has been asserted by them.
Produced by Hothouse Fiction.
www.hothousefiction.com

Cover illustration © Katie May Green, 2012

ISBN 978 1 407 13114 6

A CIP catalogue record for this book is available from the British Library.

Typeset by M Rules
Printed and bound by CPI Group (UK) Ltd, Croydon, CR0 4YY

Papers used by Scholastic Children's Books are made
from wood grown in sustainable forests.

1 3 5 7 9 10 8 6 4 2

This is a work of fiction. Names, characters, places,
incidents and dialogues are products of the author's imagination
or are used fictitiously. Any resemblance to actual people, living
or dead, events or locales is entirely coincidental.

www.scholastic.co.uk/zone

For Kitty Morrison, also affectionately
known as Granny Orkney.

And for Auriol Bussell,
the best grandma anyone could wish for.

Butterflies

Something odd was happening inside Lily Dalton's tummy. It was tumbling up and down, and round and round, making her feel a bit sick.

But Lily knew she wasn't poorly. She'd felt fine all day at school. It was only when the last bell rang and their teacher, Miss Peters, had reminded them all about

the Easter Show that Lily's tummy had begun to flutter.

"Remember it's the Easter Show tomorrow!" Miss Peters called as the class rushed to pack up their things. "You've all worked really hard and it's going to be lots of fun – just remember to smile!"

As her classmates filed out into the playground, talking excitedly, Lily stayed behind, slowly putting her things into her school bag.

"What's up, Lily?" her best friend, Antonia, asked. She already had her coat on, but she was waiting for Lily.

Lily told Antonia about her tummy. "Maybe you've got butterflies!" Antonia smiled, her brown eyes twinkling.

"*Butterflies?*" Lily asked.

Antonia gave a nod. "When my tummy flutters and I feel a bit sick, my mum says I've got butterflies in my tummy. It happens when I'm nervous."

"Oh!" Lily looked down at her stomach. So she had "butterflies". It was a nice name for a horrible feeling.

"What are you nervous about?" Antonia asked.

Lily glanced outside at the rest of their class. They were all smiling and laughing as they rushed over to meet their parents. As far as Lily could see, she was the only one feeling worried. "Nothing!" she said quickly. She couldn't say she was afraid of being on stage, not even to Antonia. Everyone else was looking forward to the show so much, they'd think she was silly for being scared. So she gave a little smile and said, "I'm excited!"

"Me too," said Antonia. "The Easter Show is going to be so much fun. My mum has bought me new tap shoes." She gave a hop as though she were already dancing.

Lily sighed. Antonia wasn't even performing in a group like Lily: she was dancing all on her own, and she wasn't scared. Lily liked singing to herself, or when she was joining in with Grandma's radio, but the thought of standing in front of an audience and singing out loud made her feel sick. What was she going to do?

"Are your mum and dad coming to watch the show?" Antonia asked as they walked out together into the playground.

Lily nodded. "And Grandma and Grandpa and my little brother Archie too."

Antonia did another little tap dance. "All my family are coming except for my puppy, Mozzie. I wish he could be there."

I wish I could stop feeling nervous, Lily thought as she waved Antonia goodbye.

Grandma and Archie were waiting for her in their usual place by the willow tree just outside the school playground. Grandma and Grandpa's house was just around the corner, and Lily and Archie went there every day after school until their mum or dad finished work and came to pick them up.

As they walked home to Grandma's house, Lily told them about the butterflies.

"It's because I'm worried about singing to an audience. My legs feel wobbly, too."

"Wibbly-wobbly legs." Archie laughed. "What if you fall down when you're singing? What if you knock everyone else down, like dominoes!"

Lily groaned. "I hadn't even thought of that."

"Stop worrying," Grandma said, gently squeezing Lily's hand. "You're not going to fall down and you're going to sing beautifully."

Lily wasn't so sure. "What if I forget all my words?" she gulped. Just thinking about it made her want to cry.

"What you need is some *confidence*," Grandma told her.

"What's a comfy dance?" Archie asked.

Grandma laughed. "Not *comfy dance*, Archie, confidence. Confidence is when you know you're good at something, and so you know you can do it," she explained.

"Like numbers?" Archie asked.

"Yes," Grandma smiled. "You know you can do your numbers now because you've practised doing them lots and lots. Practise is the way you get confidence. Like when you learn to ride a bike or swim." She gave Lily a big smile. "You can practise singing your song to us when we get home."

Grandpa was in the garden when they walked through the gate. He came towards them carrying a large basket. "I have something to show you," he said, putting the basket down on the path. Lily and Archie rushed over to look inside it. Inside were six *huge* cabbages!

Grandpa smiled proudly. "Aren't they

beautiful? It's the village vegetable competition tomorrow. My cabbages are sure to win first prize this year!"

Lily looked at his happy face. "You really feel like you can do it, don't you, Grandpa?" she asked.

Grandpa nodded. "Yes, I do, because I worked very hard to grow these cabbages. I gave them lots of love and attention." He smiled again. "*And* I have a special trick to make them grow so big and tasty."

"What trick?" Archie asked excitedly.

"It's a secret," Grandpa said. He looked around, making sure no one else could hear. Then he leaned closer and whispered, "I whistle to them."

Lily giggled. Grandpa could be so funny. Archie's face was all screwed up as he laughed. "You can't *whistle* to vegetables, Grandpa!"

"Yes I can!" Grandpa laughed. "It makes the cabbages happy and when they're happy they grow big and green. That's why I'm going to win first prize tomorrow."

"I wish I could feel like I could do my singing," Lily sighed.

"Don't worry, Lilybee." Grandpa gave her a little hug. "You'll be the star of the show. Just like my cabbages!" He picked up the basket and set off towards the greenhouse, whistling happily.

"I'm going inside," Archie said and hurried towards the house. "I've got to colour in an Easter egg for my homework."

At least someone is excited about Easter, Lily sighed, as she followed him into the kitchen. Archie sat at the kitchen table and pulled his colouring pencils and a big egg-shaped piece of card out of his school bag. Grandma started humming as she made a pot of tea. Hector the cat was curled up on the rug, licking his paws clean. They all looked happy, just like Grandpa. Lily took a deep breath. There was only one way that she could be happy too.

"I've got an announcement," she said in a clear, loud voice.

Everyone looked at her. She took a deep, shaky breath. "I'm not singing in the show."

Grandma almost dropped the teapot.

Archie's mouth fell open.

Hector stopped licking his paw.

"Are you sure, Lily?" Grandma said. "You're such a good singer. And your group is relying on you."

"I *want* to sing," Lily told her. "But I'm just *too* nervous." Her bottom lip started to quiver and she could feel a tear creeping in at the corner of each eye.

Grandma set the teapot down and came and stood in front of Lily. She tapped her fingers on the side of her mug.

"Hmmm!" she said and nodded. "Stage fright. There's only one cure."

"What cure?" Lily asked. She suddenly imagined a spoonful of nasty medicine, smelling of vinegar and tasting of prunes.

But Grandma didn't fetch any medicine. Instead she walked over to the kitchen dresser. Lily blinked away her tears and watched as Grandma stood on her tiptoes and reached up to the top shelf. Lily began to smile. *Of course!* Why hadn't she thought of it before?

A shiver ran all the way up Lily's arms, as if a gentle breeze had just circled the room. Hector meowed, but to Lily it sounded like he said, "*Magic!*" She gave an excited gasp that made Archie look up from his cardboard egg.

"What's happening?" he asked.

Lily pointed to Grandma, who was

lifting down a familiar yellow-and-white striped jar from the top shelf of the dresser. "Look!" she said, and for the first time that day, she felt a rush of happiness. "Grandma's going to open the magic jar!"

2

A Double Surprise

The first time Grandma had showed them the magic jar, Archie had been in a really bad mood. The magic jar had known just what they needed, and inside there had been a recipe for Feel Good Fairy Cakes.

Feel Good Fairy Cakes made it *impossible* to feel grumpy. As soon as Archie had eaten one, he was back to his usual cheerful self.

"I wonder what recipe will be inside the jar this time," Lily said.

Grandma set the jar down on the kitchen table. "I think you should open the jar, Lily," she said. "It's you who needs a little magic help."

Lily put her hand on the lid.

"Don't forget to make a wish!" Grandma reminded her.

Lily laid her fingers on the jar and closed her eyes. Archie put down his colouring pencils and climbed up on a chair next to her. "I'm going to wish, too," he whispered to her. "So the jar helps you like it helped me. It'll be a double wish."

"Thank you," she whispered back.

Grandma had said the jar would always give them the recipe they needed to magically make things better. *Will its magic help me sing at the Easter show?* Lily wondered.

She took a deep breath and made her wish. "I wish I could sing in front of an audience." A gentle tingling ran through her fingers. Was it magic? Lily kept her hand on the jar until the tingling stopped; she needed all the magic she could get. "*Please* help me, *please* help me," she whispered over and over again.

When she opened her eyes, Archie was staring at her. "Open it quick!" he said, jiggling impatiently. "I want to see what's inside."

Lily carefully pulled off the lid and a lovely sweet scent drifted up into the kitchen.

"Mmmm," Archie said, kneeling up on his chair for a closer look. Lily dipped her hand inside the jar and pulled out a bag of squishy marshmallows.

"Yummy!" Archie said as his eyes grew wide.

Then Lily took out a big bar of chocolate.

"Even more yummy!" Archie told her, licking his lips.

A half-full bag of Rice Krispies was the next thing to appear.

Archie looked
disappointed. "What's
magic about cereal?"

"Wait and see,"
Grandma said.
"Sometimes the
simplest things can surprise us."

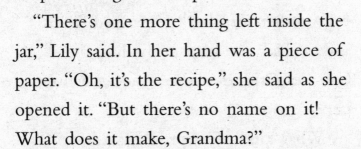

"There's one more thing left inside the
jar," Lily said. In her hand was a piece of
paper. "Oh, it's the recipe," she said as she
opened it. "But there's no name on it!
What does it make, Grandma?"

She handed it to Grandma, who
quickly read it. "I know this recipe," she
smiled. "It's for Can-Do Crispies."

Lily clapped her hands with delight.
"Can-Do Crispies. Just what I need!
Thank you, magic jar!"

Archie gazed at the bar of chocolate on
the table. "Can we make the crispies now?"

"If we're going to bake, we need to wash our hands," Grandma said. Archie quickly jumped down from the chair, ready to run over to the sink.

"Wait a moment," Grandma told him. "Before we start, I have a surprise for you both."

"Another surprise?" Lily asked. She'd already had one surprise finding the Can-Do Crispies recipe inside the magic jar.

"What kind of surprise, Grandma?" Archie asked.

Grandma gave a secret smile and pointed to where her aprons were hanging from a hook on the back of the kitchen door. "Go and choose an apron and you'll find out."

Lily and Archie rushed to the door. Grandma had lots of aprons. There was a rainbow-coloured one and a flowery one, and even one with teapots printed on it. Archie searched among them looking for one to wear, tossing them aside and making them flap around his head. "I don't know which one to choose!"

"Look!" Lily gasped. In with all the other aprons were two smaller ones she'd never seen before. They were much too small for Grandma – but they were *just* the right size for her and Archie.

"New aprons!" Archie cried. "Are they for us?"

Lily nodded. "That's the surprise!" She stood on tiptoe and lifted them down from the hook.

"The one with dinosaurs on it must be mine," Archie told her.

"Maybe it's for me." Lily teased. "Girls can have dinosaur aprons, too, you know."

Archie frowned, but then Lily giggled and draped the dinosaur apron around her little brother's neck. "Just joking – I like dinosaurs, but not as much as you do!"

"Let me help you, Archie," Grandma said. She fastened the ties at the back while Archie excitedly pointed out all the different dinosaurs on his new apron. "There's a *Dippy-docus*. . ."

"*Di*-plod-*o-cus*," Grandma reminded him, "because they *plod* along."

But Archie was too excited to listen. "And look, Grandma! A *T. Rex*!" He turned round and gave Grandma a hug. "Thank you,"

he said as he squeezed her.

Lily put on her new apron. It was yellow and white and had two pockets that looked like cupcakes. She did a twirl. "I love it," she said, and gave Grandma a big thank-you hug, too.

With a new apron and a new magic recipe, she couldn't wait to start baking!

3

Baking Magic

Grandma's cooking cupboard was one
of Lily's favourite places in the world. It
was big enough to stand inside and had
shelves stretching all the way up to the
ceiling.

Each shelf was full of delicious cooking
ingredients. There were packets of flour
and jelly and sponge fingers and bottles of
chocolate sauce. Lily and Archie called it
the Yummy Cupboard.

Every time Lily went inside it always

seemed to smell differently. Today
it smelled of lemon cake and
toffee.

"We're going to need cake cases for
our Can-Do Crispies," Grandma said,
pointing to where the cases were kept.
"Why don't you choose them, Lily?"

Lily crouched down to look at them
all. There were big ones for muffins, small
ones, flowery ones and shiny gold-and-
silver ones. There were even chocolate
ones, but Lily finally decided on some
that were a bright summery yellow.

"They look Eastery," she told Grandma.
"They're the same colour as daffodils and
fluffy chicks."

"Lovely," Grandma smiled, picking up
a tin of golden syrup from a shelf and
handing it to Archie. "Now I think we
have everything we need."

Archie couldn't wait. He hurried over to the kitchen table with the tin of syrup. Hector trotted along behind him with his little collar bell tinkling.

"Can I melt the chocolate?" Archie asked. "Lily got to do it last time."

"Yes," Grandma agreed. "But you need to break the chocolate into squares first. Do you have strong thumbs?"

"Yes!" Archie smiled, wriggling them in the air. While he got on with the job

of breaking the chocolate, Lily read out the recipe.

"We need four tablespoons of golden syrup and fifty grams of unsalted butter," she declared.

"OK. Why don't you do the butter first?" Grandma suggested. Lily carefully chopped the butter into little chunks and put them on the scales until the pointer was at fifty grams.

"Well done!" Grandma smiled, holding out a saucepan. "Now pop it into the pan."

Archie snapped off the last two squares of chocolate. "Can I melt the chocolate now?"

"First you need to put all the pieces in with the butter," Grandma told him.

He dropped the chocolate squares in, one by one. Lily liked the way they sank into the butter.

"Now it's time to add the marshmallows," Grandma told Archie. She opened the bag for him. "The marshmallows will melt quicker if you pull them into smaller pieces," she said.

"I like making this recipe," Archie said as he ripped the marshmallows apart and added them to the pan.

"Right, what do we do next?" Lily asked.

"Meow!" Hector replied from the chair next to her.

Lily giggled. "Are you going to tell me, Hector? You are the cleverest cat in the world, but you still can't read, so I'd better look for you." Lily wiped her hands on her apron and picked up the recipe. "Now we need four tablespoons of syrup."

But the lid was stuck tightly to the syrup tin. Grandma showed her how to put the tip of her spoon under the edge of the lid and push down. There was a small *pop!* as the lid came away.

Lily lifted the lid up and syrup drizzled

on to the table. "It's very sticky," She said.

"Try holding the tin over the pan," Grandma suggested. "That way the syrup won't drip everywhere."

But as soon as Lily scooped up a spoonful of syrup it slid off the spoon again! It was fun watching the syrup drip in long golden strings. It was so clear and shiny she could look right through it. She couldn't  resist sticking her finger into it and taking a taste. It was sticky on her fingers but it was smooth and soft in her mouth.

"What is syrup?" Archie asked.

"It's made from sugar and water," Grandma told him. "That's why it tastes so sweet. What's next, Lily?" she added.

Lily looked at the recipe again. "It says, 'Melt everything over a very gentle heat. Stir constantly until smooth'."

Grandma picked up the saucepan and carried it to the hob. Archie dragged a chair over to the oven and climbed up on it. "Can I stir?" he asked.

"I think I'd better do it because it's very hot," Grandma told him. "And you have to keep stirring all the time so that the mixture doesn't burn. But you can be my special helper and watch the marshmallows melt. Can you see them?"

She held the hot pan steady and gently mixed all the ingredients with a wooden spoon. "It doesn't look very delicious," Archie said as he stared into the pan.

Lily peeked in. The chocolate and the marshmallows were starting to ooze into the butter and syrup. The marshmallows left swirls of pink and white in the melting chocolate.

"They've gone all stretchy and sticky." Lily laughed. She dipped her nose close to the pan. "Mmm. It smells yummy, though!"

Hector was still sitting on a chair at the table. He gave a soft meow and twitched his nose. "Hector says he loves watching us bake," Lily giggled.

When all the ingredients had melted together and there were no more lumps, Grandma took the pan off the hob. "Follow me," she said as she carried it over to the table. "Now for the tricky part of the recipe. It's time to add the crispies."

"I'll do it!" Lily volunteered. She tipped the packet and Rice Krispies whooshed into the chocolate mixture. "Whoops!" She smiled as a few bounced off the sides of the pan and spilled on to the floor. Hector jumped down from his chair and playfully pounced on them.

"Never mind," Grandma said, giving Archie a wooden spoon. He started swishing them around, coating them in the chocolatey marshmallow mixture.

"Stir gently so that you don't crush all the crispies," Grandma told him. "Let Lily have a go."

Lily stirred the crispies extra gently, coating them in the warm chocolatey mixture. She didn't want to crush them, but they kept crackling and snapping and hissing and popping.

"It's impossible not to burst some of

them!" Lily giggled. She was having so much fun she realized she had forgotten all about her nervous tummy until Archie asked, "Can you only make Can-Do Crispies when you've got a butterflies tummy?"

"You can make Can-Do Crispies any time you need to feel brave," Grandma told him. "But since we're making them at Eastertime, I thought it would be nice to decorate them with something special."

She put her hand into the magic jar and to Lily's surprise brought out a small patterned yellow bag. Archie recognized it immediately.

"Mini Eggs!" he yelled excitedly. He stretched his arms into the air and did a little dance. "I love Easter. It's *delicious!*"

Grandma laughed but Lily didn't. She was too busy peering inside the jar.

That's funny, she thought. *I'm sure I had emptied everything out.* She put her hand inside and wiggled her fingers around. The jar was certainly empty now.

"How many crispies are we going to make? I hope it's lots!" Archie was asking. He looked longingly at the chocolate-covered cereal. Lily grinned. Grandma was right. Even boring things like cereal could be turned into something special with a little baking magic!

Lost Confidence

"We should have enough mixture to make about twelve crispies," Grandma told them as Lily and Archie got out the yellow cake cases.

Archie counted them as Lily put the cases into the tray. "We can make six crispies each," he told her, because he had got very good at counting.

Grandma said she would help them with their first crispies to show them what to do. "Take a spoonful of the mixture and put it in a cake case," she directed while helping Archie scrape the mixture off his spoon. "Then put a few Mini Eggs in the middle to make it look like a little bird's nest." She stood back and smiled. "Now you try – but be *very* careful. The marshmallows make the mixture hot."

Archie spooned so much mixture into the cake case that it spilled out over the sides.

"That's a big nest you've made," Grandma said.

"It's a nest for a *terry-dac-til*," Archie told her. "They're *flying* dinosaurs."

"Oh goodness!" Grandma smiled.

Archie placed three sugar-coated chocolate eggs inside the nest. "This one is going to be mine."

"I'm making blackbird nests," Lily said,

choosing her Mini Eggs carefully. "They have blue eggs."

Archie was making all his crispy nests as quickly as he could. "Can we eat them *now*?" he asked as he put the eggs in the last nest.

"Well . . . Can-Do Crispies are extra delicious and doubly magical when they're chilled." Grandma smiled. "But you can lick the spoons."

Archie's spoon was in his mouth before Grandma had finished speaking. "I'll pop them in the fridge and while we're waiting for them to harden, Archie can finish colouring in his Easter egg."

"Mmmm," Lily
sighed as she nibbled
the delicious warm
chocolatey crispies off
her spoon. Grandma
swept up the crispies
from the floor.
Hector had stopped
chasing after them and was curled up on
Grandpa's chair ready for a snooze.

As Lily helped Grandma tidy away, she
could hear Grandpa out in the garden
whistling a happy tune, but he stopped
suddenly when a voice called to him.

"Are you ready for the vegetable show
tomorrow?" it asked.

"Yes," Grandpa replied. "My crop of
cabbages is looking very good."

Lily was curious. She dropped her
spoon into Grandma's washing-up water

and turned to Archie. "Let's go outside and see who Grandpa is talking to."

"We can tell him about the Can-Do Crispies!" Archie said as they rushed into the garden.

The voice belonged to Mr Mellor, Grandma and Grandpa's grumpy next-door neighbour. He was standing on the other side of the garden fence. "I've just finished digging up my vegetables for the competition," Mr Mellor said, holding up a basket full of the biggest cabbages Lily had ever seen. "I've grown giants this year," he smirked. He looked so very pleased with himself that his moustache started to twitch. "They're sure to take first prize tomorrow."

Lily quickly glanced at Grandpa, who was frowning at the cabbages. She thought he looked a lot less confident now.

Mr Mellor waved goodbye. "See you tomorrow in the judging tent," he smiled smugly, "and may the best cabbages win!"

"Those were big cabbages," Grandpa said as he watched Mr. Mellor walk away. "A lot bigger than mine." Lily noticed he was rubbing his tummy.

"Don't worry, Grandpa," she whispered. "We've got just the thing for butterflies."

5

The Taste of Magic

While the crispies chilled in the fridge, Lily carefully wrote the title *Can-Do Crispies* on the top of the recipe and put it safely away in the special recipe box Grandma had

 given her. Then she picked up the box and carried it over to the dresser. Lily stared at the magic

jar, back up on the top shelf. "Please use your magic to help Grandpa, too," she whispered. "He wants his cabbages to win the vegetable show tomorrow but he's lost his can-do feeling."

Crossing her fingers tightly, Lily turned back to the kitchen table. Archie was drawing gold stars on his Easter egg. "How cold do the crispies have to be?" he asked Grandma hopefully.

"*Very* cold," Grandma said. She opened the fridge to check on them again. "They'll need five minutes more to reach their full magical effect."

"That's ages!" Archie sighed.

"Actually, it's just long enough." Grandma beckoned to Lily. "There's just enough time for Lily to practise her song."

Lily wasn't sure. "Maybe I should wait until I've eaten a Can-Do Crispy?"

"It's only me and Archie who will be listening to you." Grandma said. She pulled up a chair and settled down with a smile. "We'd love to hear you sing. We'll pretend to be the audience."

"OK," Lily said. Archie was busy colouring. If only Grandma was watching, then there was nothing to be scared of, was there? But just thinking about the word "audience" made the butterflies start fluttering again in her tummy. She walked to the middle of the kitchen floor, took a deep breath and began to sing.

"I'm going on an egg hunt, where can they be?"

* **

As Lily sang, she raised her hand to her eyes as if she were looking out for eggs. Grandma smiled and nodded.

"*Under the garden hedge or in the apple tree?*"

She pointed up to the ceiling as if there were a tall tree growing in the kitchen.

"*I'll look inside the watering can and behind the flower pots,*"

She started to do a twirl, but she lost her balance and stumbled. "Whoa!" she cried as she bumped into Archie's chair. Archie knocked his pencil case on the floor, and pens and pencils crash-landed next to Hector, who gave a startled yowl and hid under the table.

"Sorry, Archie! Sorry, Hector!" Lily cried.

"Never mind," Grandma said cheerfully,

scooping up all the pens and pulling Hector on to her lap for a stroke. "Keep going." But Lily shook her head. She couldn't do it.

"Why don't you start again, from the beginning?" Grandma said. "You're very good at twirling. I'm sure you won't bump into anyone at the show."

With Grandma's encouragement, Lily started to sing again. This time she only got as far as the first line before she stopped. "Oh no! I forgot to point to the apple tree!" she wailed. "I'm never going to get it right!"

Archie looked at Grandma. "I think Lily needs a magic crispy right now."

Grandma agreed. "You do look a bit flustered, Lily. Why don't you sit down while I pour you a nice glass of milk?"

Lily followed Grandma to the fridge.

While Grandma poured the milk, she checked on the Can-Do Crispies. She prodded the extra big dinosaur crispy nest with her finger. The chocolate was hard and the little eggs were stuck fast inside the nest. They looked delicious. She just hoped they would work.

"They're ready!" she confirmed. Grandma pulled them out of the fridge and put them on the kitchen table. Lily and Archie scrambled into their seats.

"We should ask Grandpa if he would like one," Lily said, taking a gulp of milk. "He needs confidence, too."

Archie marched outside and stood on the doorstep. He cupped a hand either side of his mouth and called out across the garden, "Grandpa! Come and get your Comfy Dance!"

When everyone was sitting round the kitchen table, Grandma handed out the crispies.

"We can all have two," Archie counted. "And there are two each for Mummy and Daddy as well. But that's my one." He pointed to the dinosaur nest. "It's the biggest and the best."

"Just because something is big it doesn't mean it's the best, Archie," Lily corrected him. She was worried about Grandpa. He had stopped whistling after seeing the enormous cabbages Mr Mellow was entering in the vegetable show.

"I'm eating the little chocolate eggs first," Archie was saying now. There was a hard crunching sound as a sugar-coated egg was crushed between his teeth.

Lily handed Grandpa one of the nests. "It's called a Can-Do Crispy," she told him.

"It looks delicious," he said.

She watched him take a bite. Then another. How long before the magic started to work and Grandpa felt like he could win the vegetable show again?

"Aren't you going to eat yours, Lily?" Grandma asked.

Lily took a bite. The crispy was chocolatey and very cold. The rice cereal seemed to pop in her mouth with each bite. *They were exploding and chasing away the butterflies away.* She took another bite. The marshmallow and the syrup made them chewy as well as crunchy. They were so delicious she was glad there were two each. By the time she finished eating her second crispy, she felt happy and ready for anything!

Archie had finished his crispies too. "Has it worked, Lily?" he asked. "Are you going to be in the show?" He had a bit of chocolate at the corner of his mouth and on his fingertips.

"I think so," she said.

"There's only one way to find out for sure," Grandma said. "Sing your song for us, Lily."

A magical thing happened. Lily didn't feel nervous at all! When everyone pulled up their chairs and sat down and stared at her expectantly, she calmly took her place in the middle of the floor. Her legs weren't wobbly either. She took a deep breath and began to sing:

"*I'm going on an egg hunt. . .*"

This time she remembered the words and all the different actions and even ended her song with a perfect twirl.

Everyone clapped. "Well done, Lilybee!" Grandpa cheered.

"The Can-Do Crispies worked!" she said. "I wasn't nervous at all!"

But then Lily had a horrible thought. She looked down at the crumbs on her plate in despair. "Oh no! I haven't got any Can-Do Crispies left! What if the magic wears off by tomorrow?"

"Don't worry," said Grandma. "The magic will definitely last until after the show. And you should be confident – you just sang it *perfectly*."

Lily smiled and turned to Grandpa. "Remember to eat a Can-Do Crispy before the vegetable competition. Then you won't be worried. They really do work," she said. "I was nervous until I ate them and now I can't *wait* to sing in the Easter show!"

6

The Easter Show

The next day at school, everyone was rushing around the classroom, putting on their costumes and excitedly getting ready for the show.

Everyone had different costumes depending on what they were doing in the show. Lily's group were all dressed as Easter bunnies, with floppy felt ears, grey t-shirts and whiskers painted on their faces. Some of their fluffy cotton-wool tails were already starting to fall off and

Miss Peters was busily sticking them back on.

"I wish I could be a lion instead of a rabbit," Lily's friend Charlie complained as Miss Peters glued his tail.

"You don't get Easter lions," she told him.

He shrugged and gave a roar anyway. "Guess what?" he growled.

"What?" Lily asked.

"The teachers are putting even more seats out in the hall. There are going to be *hundreds* of people at the show! Come and see!"

Charlie hopped over to the curtain. Lily followed him and peered through. When she looked out at the rows of empty chairs in the hall and imagined them full of people staring at her, she felt her legs start to wobble.

There's no need to be nervous, Lily told herself. *I've practised lots and I know all the words and all the actions.*

But just then the hall doors opened and lots of parents and grandparents started arriving in the hall. Lily clutched her tummy.

"What's wrong?" Antonia asked.

Lily turned and looked at her friend. She was dressed as an Easter chick. She was wearing a yellow T-shirt and yellow skirt and she had an orange cardboard beak covering her nose. Yellow tissue-paper wings hung from her arms.

"Are you poorly?" Antonia asked. Lily shook her head and closed the curtain. "I was feeling really excited about the show after I had a Can-Do Crispy, but now I'm getting nervous again!"

Antonia frowned. "What's a Can-Do Crispy?" she asked.

"It's magic." Lily sighed. "They're made of chocolate and crispies and marshmallows. They stop you being worried." Then she gasped. She had forgotten to keep how scared she felt a secret.

But Antonia didn't laugh. Instead she said, "Do you think *I* could have a Can-Do Crispy? I've got butterflies in my tummy."

Lily stared at her. "Are you nervous, too?"

Antonia nodded. "A little. My tap

shoes are new. I'm worried I might slip. I wish my dog Mozzie was here. I don't feel nervous when he watches me dance."

Lily held her Antonia's hand. "Don't worry. You've practised lots and you're really good at tap-dancing. You can do it!"

"You can as well, Lily." Antonia squeezed her hand.

Lily nodded. She knew she could – but she wished the butterflies would remember that!

Lily gulped as she looked at the clock on the wall. It was almost time to go into the hall. "Is everyone in their groups?" Miss Peters asked. "Make sure you have everything with you." She gathered Lily's group of bunnies together. "Good luck," she said with a smile.

Everyone had started to line up when

there was a knock at the door. "Come in!" Miss Peters called out.

Lily peered out from behind Charlie's wobbly bunny ears and stared at the door.

The door opened and Grandma rushed in looking very flustered. Her cheeks were pink, her hair was ruffled and she was breathless, but she was carrying a large cake box.

What was Grandma doing back here? Lily tried to ask her but Grandma just gave a secretive smile and hurried over to talk with Miss Peters. Lily watched as Grandma removed the box lid and Miss Peters looked inside it. She clapped her hands and turned to the class. "Lily's grandma has brought us all a lovely surprise. Come and see."

Everybody crowded round and peered inside the box. There were lots of delighted gasps. The box was full of lovely little chocolate nests filled with sugar-covered eggs.

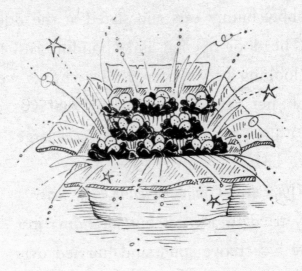

"Can-Do Crispies!" Lily grinned. "Thanks, Grandma – that's just what we need!"

A Very Friendly Audience

As her class crowded round the cake box, Lily proudly explained about the Can-Do Crispy magic. "They stop you feeling nervous," she told them.

Everyone wanted to taste one. Everyone said they had butterflies. Even Miss Peters said she needed one. Luckily, Grandma had brought enough crispies for them all.

The crispies were so delicious that the noisy classroom soon grew quiet. All that could be heard were happy sighs and the crunch of crispies being munched.

"Good luck with your song," Grandma whispered to Lily. "You're going to be brilliant."

"Thanks, Grandma." Lily took another bite of her crispy and gave a big chocolatey grin. "I'll be fine now."

The magic soon began to work. Everyone in the class was talking at once, saying, "I don't feel nervous at all. . . My butterflies have gone. . . Can I have another crispy. . .?"

As Grandma left to go and watch the show, everyone thanked her for the crispies. "They were delicious," Antonia said, and she flapped her paper wings. "And I feel like I can do anything."

"So do I!" Lily said. *In fact*, she thought as they waited to go onstage, *I am really excited about singing!*

Lily could hear the audience clapping and laughing. It sounded as if there were a lot of people out there, but she didn't feel scared at all. Not even when Miss Peters said in a loud whisper, "It's our turn now. Dancers on stage first, please."

Everyone who was dressed as an Easter chick filed onstage. Miss Peters introduced the act as "Antonia and the chicks".

"Good luck," Lily whispered as Antonia tippety-tapped her way onstage.

The music started. Lily peeked through the curtain and saw the chicks doing lots of flapping actions that made their paper wings flutter up and down. Then Antonia started to dance. *Clickety clickety* went her new tap shoes as she skipped and twirled and jumped and swayed. Her feet moved so fast that when she stretched out her arms, she looked as if she were about to fly away.

Lily thought it was the best Antonia had ever danced. The audience must have thought so too, because when the dance finished, they clapped very loudly and cheered. Antonia couldn't stop smiling. Neither could Lily. She watched Antonia wave to her mum, dad and three sisters in the audience before skipping back to where the rest of the class were waiting. The audience was still clapping as the last of the chicks flapped offstage.

"Well done," Lily whispered to Antonia. "You were brilliant!"

"And I didn't slip on my new shoes!" Antonia beamed.

"Bunnies, get ready," Miss Peters said. "It's time for your song. It's the last part of the show, so remember to sing loudly and clearly."

Lily followed the rest of her group on

to the stage. The lights were bright, so she had to stare into the audience to look for her family. Just as the music started she spotted Mum and Dad, Archie, Grandma and Grandpa all sitting in the front row. Mum and Grandma cheered and Archie waved. Lily gave a little wave back.

The hall became very quiet as Miss Peters thanked everyone for coming to watch the show. "The next act is a song called 'The Egg Hunt'. We hope you enjoy it."

Mr Adams, the music teacher, started to play the piano. *Pompity pompity pomm pomm* went the music. Lily opened her mouth ready to sing. Her legs didn't feel wobbly at all. She took a deep breath and started to sing along with the rest of her group.

"I'm going on an egg hunt. . ."

Their voices soared across the hall. Lily felt so happy that her voice was the loudest of them all. She remembered all her words perfectly and threw out her arms for her hand actions. She even remembered to look at the audience and found they were smiling back at her. Some were even tapping their feet, while others were swaying in their seats. Lily grinned. They liked the song!

"*I'll look inside the watering can and behind the flower pots,*

I'll crawl beneath the summer seat and between the rhubarb stalks. . ."

When the song finished, the audience burst into applause. Everyone in the class was meant to take a bow, then hop off stage, but Lily was so happy that she also did a curtsy, and then she did an extra twirl as well.

"Hooray!" she heard Grandpa call out above the applause. He and Grandma were smiling and clapping and looking very happy. He must have remembered to eat a Can-Do Crispy too, Lily thought to herself.

Archie was clapping too, although it was difficult with a toy dinosaur in his hand. Mum and Dad were looking as if they were never going to stop clapping. "More!" yelled the audience. "More! More!"

Lily waved again and did another twirl until Miss Peters beckoned her off the stage.

Audiences weren't scary after all, Lily decided as she gave her family a final wave. In fact, they were very, very friendly.

8

The Star of the Show

When the show was finished, Miss Peters told them it was the best one ever.

"It must have been the Can-Do Crispies," Lily smiled.

Miss Peters agreed. "They certainly helped *you* to sing loud and clear, Lily. You were the star of the show! Well done, everyone."

Everyone chattered excitedly as they waited for their families to come and pick them up. Antonia's mum came to the classroom to collect her. She was carrying a squirming little black puppy in her arms.

"It's Mozzie!" Antonia squealed with delight and hurried over to cuddle him.

"He was allowed to sit outside the hall," her mum told her. "I'm sure he could hear you dance." She turned to Lily and smiled. "And I'm sure he could hear your lovely singing. We all could! You were a star!"

Lily grinned until her face started to ache. She was still smiling as her family

came and got her and they all went
to Grandma and Grandpa's house for
afternoon tea.

"Were you supposed to do so many
curtsies and twirls?" Archie asked her.

Lily giggled. "I like twirling," she said
and twirled again. "Did you all enjoy the
show?"

"Oh, yes," Grandma told her. "I didn't
know you could sing so loud!"

"It was the Can-Do Crispies," Lily
told her. "They made me want to sing so
people at the back of the hall could hear."

"Oh, I think people in Australia could
hear you," Grandpa joked.

Lily giggled – but gasped as she stepped
into the kitchen. Sitting on the kitchen
table was Grandpa's basket of cabbages,
and pinned to it was a big red first-prize
rosette.

"Grandpa!" she cried. "You won!"

Grandpa gave a big proud smile. "Yes," he said. "Mr Mellor's cabbages were bigger, but the judges said mine were tastier."

"Then your cabbages *were* the best! You were the star of the show, too!" Lily hugged Grandpa tight.

"That's because you whistled to them, isn't it, Grandpa?" Archie said.

"Yes," Grandpa said. "And next year I'm going to grow carrots and I'm going to whistle to them so they'll win first prize as well!"

Lily picked up the red rosette and pinned it to his jacket. "You're a champion Grandpa, too," she said. "I'm glad the crispies gave you back your confidence."

"If you know you can do something really well, then there's no need to be nervous," Grandpa told her. "Whether it's growing cabbages or singing."

"But having Can-Do Crispies helps." Grandma smiled. "In fact, I think we should celebrate with another crispy!"

Archie's hand shot up. "Yes, please. I could eat them all day."

"Don't have too many," Lily said with a giggle. "I think I had a little *too much* can-do feeling when I was singing my song." She glanced up to the top shelf of the dresser. "Thank you, magic jar," she whispered.

"Sing your song again, Lily!" Mum said.

Lily looked at Grandpa. "Will you whistle along with me?"

So Lily sang and Grandpa whistled. Mum, Dad and Grandma clapped along while Archie crunched a sugar-coated chocolate egg in time to the music. And Hector must have been feeling happy as well, because he jumped up on a chair and purred so loudly, it sounded as if he was singing, too.

Look out for more

Bake a Wish

books

Bake a Wish

Feel Good Fairy Cakes

Includes FANTASTIC cut-out-and-keep recipe card!

Lorna Honeywell

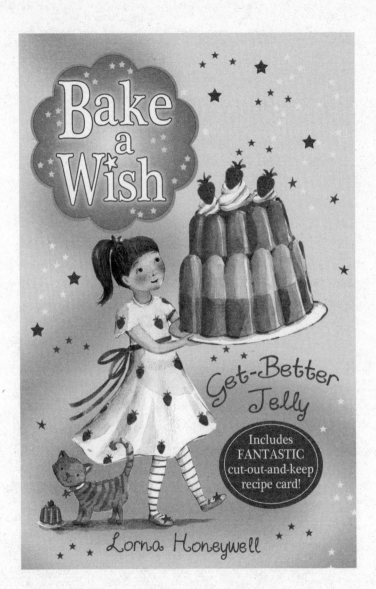

Bake a Wish

Get-Better Jelly

Includes FANTASTIC cut-out-and-keep recipe card!

Lorna Honeywell

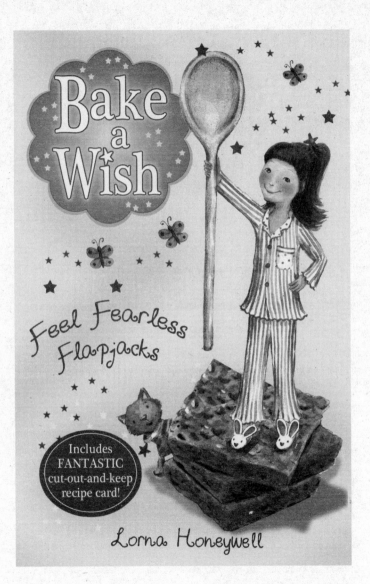

Bake a Wish

Feel Fearless Flapjacks

Includes FANTASTIC cut-out-and-keep recipe card!

Lorna Honeywell

For more baking
fun and extra
recipes visit

www.scholastic.co.uk/zone